GORDON'S
GREAT ESCAPE

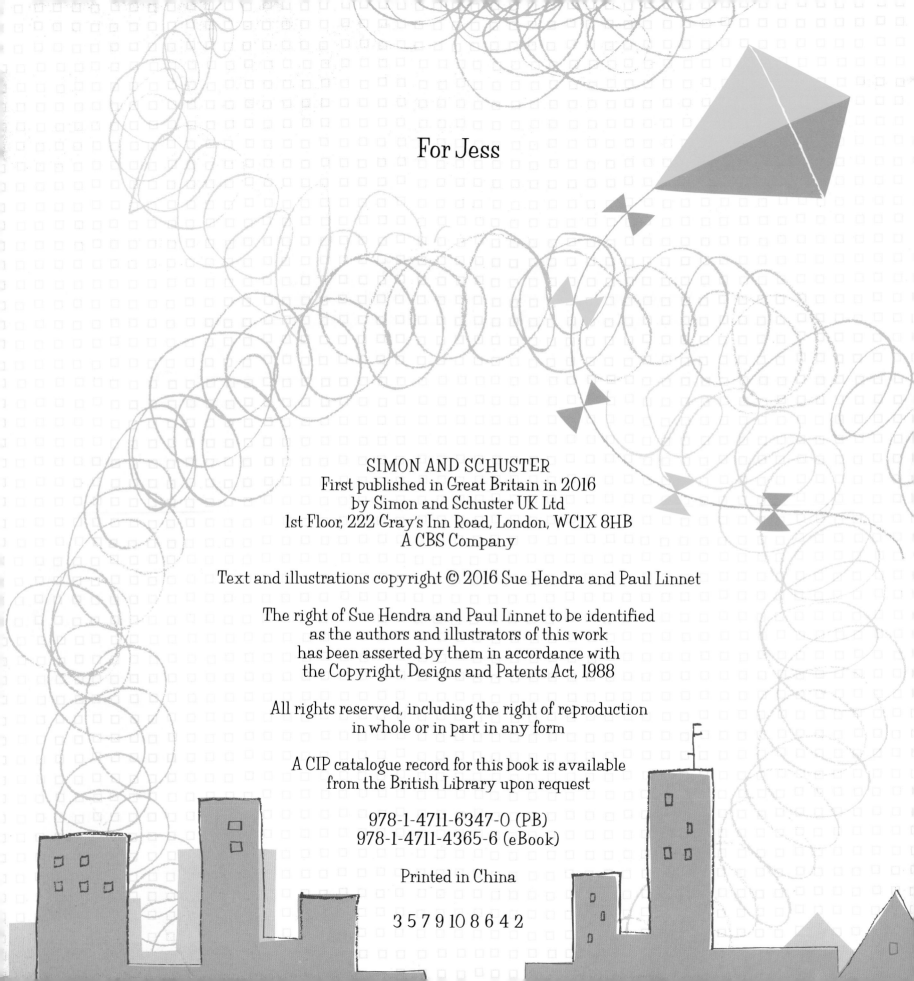

For Jess

SIMON AND SCHUSTER
First published in Great Britain in 2016
by Simon and Schuster UK Ltd
1st Floor, 222 Gray's Inn Road, London, WC1X 8HB
A CBS Company

A CIP catalogue record for this book is available
from the British Library upon request

978-1-4711-6347-0 (PB)
978-1-4711-4365-6 (eBook)

Printed in China

3 5 7 9 10 8 6 4 2

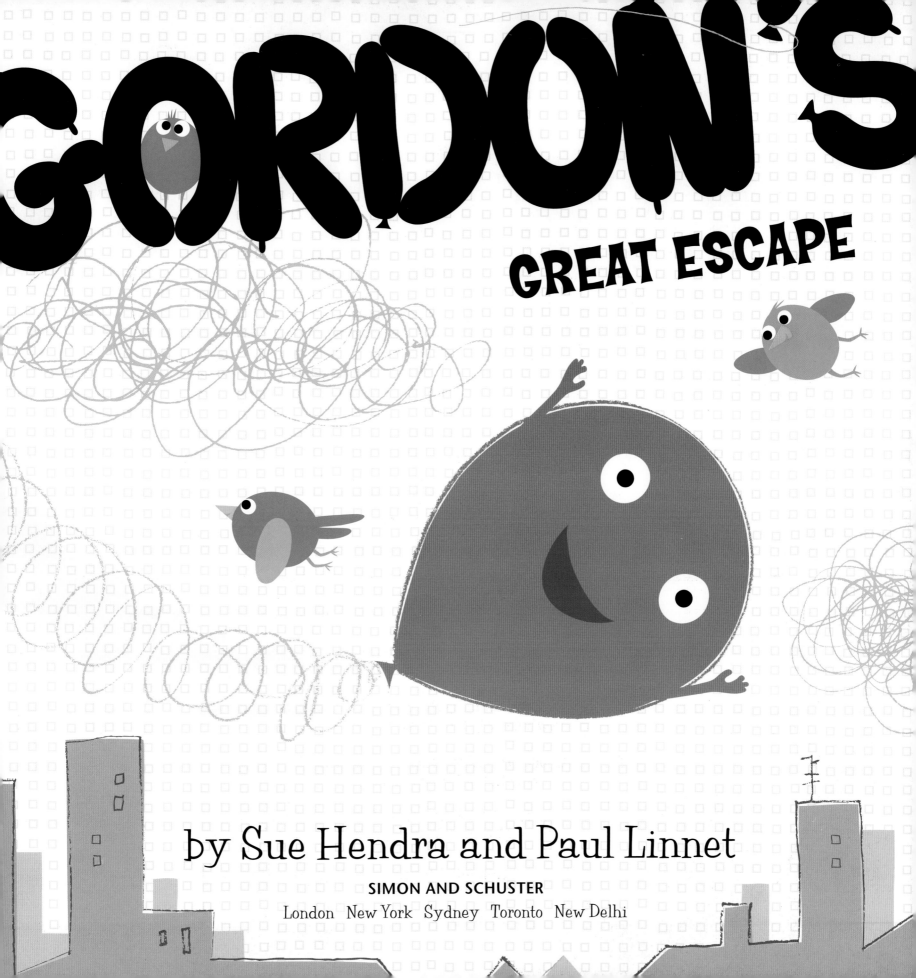

GORDON'S
GREAT ESCAPE

by Sue Hendra and Paul Linnet

SIMON AND SCHUSTER
London New York Sydney Toronto New Delhi

This is Gordon. He's a balloon!

You may think being a balloon
is all about parties and floating about.

Well, not for Gordon, as you will see.

This is his story.
It starts a long, long time ago . . .

. . . when Gordon was little and still in his packet.

As time went on he grew,

and grew,

until he was big enough for . . .

... balloon school!

Here he is, learning some important lessons.

Before long it was time for his first party.
He was a little bit shy but he had a brilliant time.

And that's when he met Penelope.

They thought they'd be together forever.

She took him to the seaside
to make sandcastles.

She took him to the park
to play on the swing.

Then at last she took him
home to meet . . .

...her pet porcupines!

"ARGH! Prickles!" shouted Gordon and with a huge **pfffft!** he escaped out of the window . . .

... and slap bang into a **magic show!**

He became the
magician's assistant.

It was great!

Until the finale.

"I just need to POP the balloon in my magic bag!" she said.

POP?!

ARGH! thought Gordon.

And with a huge
pffffft! he escaped . . .

. . . into a BIG stripy tent.

And that's when his life in the circus began.

Oh, how he loved being a circus balloon.
He wasn't at all scared of heights.

And he loved to make
people laugh.

Together he and his circus friends
travelled the world.

But one fateful day they were caught in a storm . . .

. . . and their ship sank!

They thought they would never be rescued, so Gordon bravely went for help.

"My friends have never let me down –
so I can't let THEM down!" he said,
as he flew through wind and rain.

Finally he had to admit that he was lost.
How would he ever find help now?

As luck would have it, help found him!

Together they rescued
Gordon's friends . . .

. . . and headed back for dry land.

A crowd of people – even the mayor –
had gathered to meet the brave
little balloon.

It was a celebration!

"In honour of your bravery, I would like to present you with this medal," said the mayor.

YIKES!

Could Gordon make one last escape?

BANG! BANG! BANG!

"Fireworks! I LOVE fireworks," said Gordon.
He was so happy, he could

BURST!